My Daddy and Me

Malgosia Piatkowska   Sam Hilton

ARCTURUS

My Daddy is very special.

We do lots of fun things together.

For breakfast, we both like to eat

Draw a picture of you and Daddy making breakfast together.

My best friend is ....

Draw a picture of you and your best friend together.

When he was my age, Daddy's best friend was

....

When I am outside, I like playing

....

Daddy likes playing ....

Show you and Daddy outside together here.

The thing I most like to bake is

....

Daddy likes to bake ....

Stick the recipe for Daddy's number one treat here.

My best TV show is

....

The song I love to sing is

Draw a character from your show in the TV.

Daddy's number one TV show is

....

Daddy's top song is

....

Use this box to show you and Daddy singing and dancing.

At the park, I love to play on

....

When he was my age, Daddy loved to play on

....

Draw a picture of you and Daddy at the playground.

The animal I like best is

....

The animal Daddy likes best is ....

Show the animals saying hello
to each other here.

The toy I play with most often is

....

The toy Daddy likes is ....

....

Draw a picture of you and Daddy playing a game together.

Inside this wallet is a card for Daddy.
Can you make it special for him? Here are some ideas!

- Write "To Daddy" inside the card.
- Draw him a picture.
- Sign your name at the bottom.
- Add kisses by writing "X."
- Put the card inside the envelope and write his name on the front.

Give the card to Daddy to show him how much you love him.